# OH BOY !

D. M. MANNIX.

# INTRODUCTION

This is the story of a young man's coming of age, and all that entails, including his old fashioned father's reactions to the related events.

# CHAPTER 1

It did happen, but only on a Wednesday. Raymond O'Keeffe as always on leaving work on a Wednesday stopped off at the club on William Street for a sociable game of bridge. He is a pleasant enough man to play with, as he knows the game well and he always knows how to make the most of the hand he's been dealt. If his partner Jeff makes an error Raymond can always be counted on to find an excuse for him.

Therefore, it is surprising on this Wednesday to hear him verbally lacerate his partner with undeserved sharpness and it is even more surprising when Raymond makes a grave error on the next hand, an error no one would have ever thought that Raymond would make.

Jeff, who was still trying to get a little bit of his dignity back, decided he has to point out Raymond's stupid error to the group, and he deliberately does it so loudly that everyone in the room, not just the four of them sitting at the table heard him. Now, the four of them sitting around the table are old buddies and they have been playing this Wednesday ritual for years, so none of them took Raymond's bad humour and bad card playing too seriously.

Raymond is a broker of good standing for many year's and he is also a full partner in a highly respected brokerage in the city. So it occurred to them that something must have gone really wrong at work, maybe with the stock he is working on today……

'How was work today?' Jeff ventured, trying to get him to open up….. 'oh great,' Raymond told them, 'even mugs are capable of making money today.'

So stock's and share's it seems aren't the reason for Raymond's bad mood…. so what is the reason? Raymond was a chap who seemed to always enjoy good health and financially he was quite comfortable, and that fact was a testament to his good judgment, preceding the stock market crash of a few years ago. Raymond had a great family life and he loved his wife Susan, and his children Leanne and Jack very much. So as a rule, Raymond didn't do grumpy, he usually laughed easily at any nonsense they were apt to talk about while playing.

But today he was just sitting there looking glum, even his bulky eyebrows that looked pretty ferocious on a normal day, looked seriously puckered, and his mouth had dropped into a sulky expression. In order to ease the tension at the table, one of his other card playing pals mentioned the one subject they all knew Raymond would be happy to speak about, it might even pull him out of his black mood.

'Well Raymond, I see your boy performed well in that last tennis competition,' Jeff ventured, but the expression on Raymond's face grew even darker 'he's done no better than was expected,' he replied in a grumpy voice.

'So when do you expect Jack to get home?'

'He got home late last night.'

'Oh, that's great, and did he say that he had enjoyed himself?' Jeff enquired, 'yes, he did but all I know about it is that he's made a total fool of himself.'

'Did he! how did he manage to do that?' Jeff enquired.

So, Raymond barked back 'I'm not saying okay.'

At this his three mates looked over at him, curiosity is written all over their faces, Raymond just scowled silently at the green baize on the card table.

'Sorry Raymond, your call,' Brian cautiously informed him.

The game went on but it continued in a strained silence. This time Raymond got his bid but his next move was to play his hand of cards so badly that him and Jeff went three down. No one said a word around the table, and there was a heavy silence as they looked at Jeff waiting for another outburst from him.

Another rubber began. This time Raymond's first move was to deny a suit. 'You're having none!' Kyle gasped incredulously, Raymond didn't reply, he didn't even bother looking up from his hand of cards. And at the end of the hand it appeared that this revoke had cost them the rubber.

Kyle could not let it pass without a comment…. 'What the hell's the matter with you tonight O'Keeffe you're playing like a damn fool for God's sake.' This comment really vexed Raymond, and hard and all as he tried, he couldn't seem to pull himself out of the black mood he had found himself in. It was one thing him losing the big rubber but the fact that his partner would speak to him like this and while they were still at the table, well that did require some sort of action.

'Listen,' Raymond started 'I guess I'd better withdraw. I had thought that a few rubbers would help to calm my mind, but to tell you the truth it's not working and I am still in a foul temper.' His buddies burst out laughing at this revelation, 'and you're actually telling us this! If you don't mind me saying it's sort of obvious' Jeff retorted.

Robert gave them a rueful sort of a smile....... 'okay and I'll bet any of you would be in a bit of a temper if Jack was your son, it's really put me in an awkward position. So if any of you could give me some useful advice on how to deal with this problem, I'd be very grateful.'

'Let's get a drink and you can tell us all about it okay. Between the three of us, well, if we can't advise you how to deal with any situation, then surely nobody can' Kyle remarked. *Yes, he's right,* Raymond thought, *with a Solicitor, a Civil servant who worked in the Law Department, a Teacher, and myself, we should be able to come up with a workable solution for just about any problem.*

So, Kyle walked over to the wall and solemnly pressed the bell for the waiter.

'It's that damned boy of mine,' Raymond continued in a quiet voice.

They ordered drinks and they were served to them had them at the bar, drinking slowly as the story continued...... the boy whom Raymond spoke of is his only son, Jack, and he's eighteen years old now. Raymond and Susan also have two lovely daughters, Leanne and Rosie, Leanne is seventeen years of age and Rosie is fifteen two years younger. Both of them are good students and were also eager to help their mother out at home.

As hard as Raymond tried not to show his true feelings, there was no doubt in anyone's mind that the bigger share of his affection was held in reserve for his only son Jack. To anyone observing them he always seemed to be loving and considerate to all three his children, but it was in a more restrained, conservative sort of way with his daughters.

He did realise this and he always made sure to give handsome and expensive presents on their birthdays, and also on any other occasion that might present itself.

Raymond truly doted on his only son and Jack in turn, played along to his father's tune knowing full well that all he has to do is mention having a desire for something, maybe the latest games console, and it will arrive home a day or two later under his dad's arm. Nothing it seems is too good or too expensive for jack, when Jack is in the room Raymond can hardly take his eyes off of him. Then again Jack was the type of son any parent could be proud of, by the time he was sixteen years of age he stood nearly six feet tall, he was lithe, while at the same time was a muscular young man, who had broad shoulders a slim waist and an erect posture. And all of this was topped off with thick rust coloured hair, that sat proudly on his head, it had a natural kink and it was the perfect colour to set off his big blue eyes with those curly long dark lashes, under his definite eyebrows. His skin always seemed to have a healthy glow, no matter the time of year. And then there's his full red lips, his smile revealed a set of perfect snow-white teeth that hadn't needed orthodontic braces to correct.

Jack certainly isn't a shy boy, but he wasn't the type to be in your face either, there was modesty in his demeanour, and that was very attractive, or so his father believed. Jack had been sent to a good school, and the results of which were at least in Raymond's opinion, an engaging specimen of a young man. Raymond also believed, his one and only son showed he was the offspring of nice, normal, healthy parents, and came from a nice, normal, healthy home.

When Jack reached fourteen he had started to develop a natural talent for lawn tennis. So, when Raymond discerned in his son the promise of an excellent tennis player, he fostered it as much as he possibly could. He had Jack coached by the best, and he was so proud of him, Jack stood nearly six feet tall and it seems he had all the required attributes, he was tall and had a long reach, he was quick on his feet and his timing, well it was just perfect. He seemed to instinctively know where the ball was going to land, and it seems he was somehow always in the right spot to return it. Jack quickly began developing serious strength in his shoulders, and became quicker around the court He had a powerful serve and it came with a nasty break that made it very difficult for his opponent to return, and just to improve on all of this, his forehand drive was long and low, as well as being accurate and deadly.

As a result of this Jack started winning number of fairly major inter-county tournaments.

## CHAPTER 2

By the time Jack turned eighteen, his plan was to go to University in Dublin. However, Raymond knew that Jack was just not up to the standard required for University tennis. Even though he had started winning tournaments his backhand and his volleying were still a wee bit all over the court. So once again, the best coach that Raymond could find was got for him, the cost didn't seem to matter.

Finally, Jack went off to Dublin, to the more established UCD University College Dublin, rather than the newer DCU Dublin City University and his dad honestly believed that he had instilled the idea that his son could play for the UCD tennis team firmly in Jack's head, before he had even left the house to go to Colbert Station to catch the train to Dublin. And he also quietly cherished his ultimate ambition, to see his son play at the big Wimbledon Tournament in the summer. A lump would start forming in Raymond's throat whenever he pictured his boy Jack leaping over the net to shake the hand of the American champion he had just thrashed in three straight sets, just like the great McEnroe used to. And then, to nonchalantly walk off the Centre Court in triumph to the deafening plaudits of his fans.

Now Raymond had many friends in the world of tennis, and one evening after he stayed late in the city for a business dinner, he found himself in the Tennis Club bar. And he was sitting next to Jonathan Brisbane at the bar. Raymond only vaguely knew him but he was aware that Jonathan Brisbane was one of the selectors for the National Tennis Association. So Raymond introduced himself and the two of them began chatting about the day's news. Raymond coyly guided the topic of conversation to tennis. He got stuck into him and told Jonathan in effusive terms all about Jack and his talent for tennis.

After about 5 minutes of Raymond's incessant talk, Jonathan Brisbane raised his right hand and placed his palm in front of Raymond's face, Raymond stopped talking and took a much needed sip from his glass of beer.

'Okay, so why don't you let him go up to Fitzwilliam Tennis Club and play in their next tournament?' Jonathan asked. 'I don't think he's good enough for that, and he's not nineteen yet' Raymond told him, 'and, I'm sure he wouldn't stand a chance up there with all of those Dublin lads.' 'Of course a lot of the Dublin lads, who have been playing tennis, some since before they could walk, probably would pulverize him. But Jack should be well able to play well against a lot of them, and some, if he's as good as you're saying, he may even beat, and he'd learn a lot more doing that, then he'll ever learn playing in the provincial tournaments you're currently entering him into' and Johnathan Brisbane was smiling as he swallowed a mouthful of his drink. Raymond knew he would be pondering these words of advice for the next few days.

Jonathan went on to ask Raymond when the school term was due to end. 'Oh Jack has just started at UCD so I'm not too sure, but I will find out and let you know and one more thing, I will be eternally grateful if you could somehow get him into the Fitz-William Tennis Club. Although it must not interfere with his College work, because

I've always impressed on him that tennis is a game and it mustn't interfere in any way with work or study.' Jonathan asked him if there were any holidays or term breaks coming up, and Raymond assured him he would find out and let him know.

So, they finished their chat with a promise to stay in contact, and Raymond headed home feeling very please with himself, as he now had an actual team selector's phone number and email address in his pocket. He felt so elated by this, that as soon as he got home he blurted it all out, word for word to Susan, and in a voice that sounded an octave or two higher than usual. 'Gosh, that's great Raymond' Susan told him, 'fancy Jonathan Brisbane thinking Jack is as good as that.'

It came as a big surprise to Raymond when Susan was so approving and it came as an even bigger surprise that she actually knew who Jonathan Brisbane was and what he actually does.

Susan went on in her matter of fact voice, 'now that Jack is 18, why he's practically an adult and he has never caused any real bother, and there's no reason to think that he is going to start now.'

Raymond in an unusual tone of voice interjected ......... 'but his studies, don't forget about those and I'm sure it will set a very bad precedent to let him miss days just to play tennis, this early in his academic career,' and there is something so irritatingly self centred about the way Raymond said this, it was as if his opinion was the only opinion that could possibly be if any importance.

'Oh Raymond, you have already spent a lot of time as well as a lot of our money on getting Jack ready for just this sort of opportunity, and now this! You're putting silly obstacles in front of him, what harm will it do to miss a few days of college? It seems a shame to rob him of a chance like this, and if I know my son and I think I do, I'm quite sure he'll jump at it.' It seemed to Susan that her husband was satisfied just to have been vindicated in this way. Raymond sighing deeply pondered on what his wife had just said…. 'no Susan, I've made up my mind and I'm not going to change it.' Susan held her peace because she knew her husband well enough to know what buttons needed to be pressed, and Susan had a plan….. And she set about implementing it the very next morning, as soon as Raymond left for work Susan called her son. His phone had to ring about 10 times before in a fairly groggy voice he answered, *so he isn't gone to College yet*….. Then, when she had his full attention she told him what she would do if she were in his shoes and wanted to go to to Fitzwilliam Tennis Club, she also told him not to pay too much attention when his father start's moaning and seems to be saying the opposite of what he has been saying for years. Jack was smiling to himself as he thought *here she is giving me a way to do this without hurting dad too much, she really put's up with a lot from him.* 'Thanks mum, I'll think about it and see what needs to be done, now don't be worrying yourself okay, I will call Dad when I have a plan, just don't say a word to him about this call, okay, I will call Dad when I've a plan and Mum thanks again, I really appreciate you telling me this.' A day later Raymond received a call from his son and his exuberant excitement was evident even over the phone. Jack gleefully told Raymond that he had spoken to his main tutor, who was also the Provost at the College, and as it happens the Provost was also an avid Tennis player himself. And to make matters even better, the Provost also happened to know Jonathan Brisbane and he had a high opinion of his views on Tennis players. The Provost had said to him that this was too good an opportunity to miss, and he could leave before the end of term with no repercussions. So, Jack asked his father if he could go to Fitzwilliam Tennis Club, and he faithfully promised that he'd work like the blazes all the next term, and his parents would be so proud of him it would all be worth it. Raymond was silent for a few moments then he began, 'I'm not too sure I should allow you to skip college to go to Fitzwilliam to play tennis, but as you said, the provost thinks it's an opportunity that shouldn't be missed. So, I will concede this one time, and I only hope that you can be sensible. There are a a few things I want to warn you about, so please realize that I'm telling you this for your own good.' 'Okay dad I'm listening, and I promise I won't let you down.' So, Raymond began, 'well, there will be a lot of young women there, all scantily dressed in their tennis whites. You are to have nothing to do with them, as your studies will suffer. The next one is gambling. While it may seem like great fun, don't gamble, I have seen too many men, young and old one's end up in the gutter, penniless, so do not gamble. And finally, don't lend money to anyone, not even €50. Now, if you can remember those three things, then you won't cone to any real harm. You see Jack I've been around a lot longer than you, and I know this world pretty well, so believe me this is good advice.' 'I know dad and I won't forget it, I promise.' So, over the next three days Jack finished up any lingering assignments for his remaining classes, then he started a new type of journey over at Fitzwilliam Tennis Club. He finished his first match, and he didn't disgrace himself, then he went on to snatch an unexpected victory over one of the seeded players, in a match that ended up being a lot closer than anyone had thought possible, and in the doubles, he actually got as far as the semi-finals with his partner. In the Clubhouse afterward it was the general view that he showed a lot of promise and also his natural charm would conquer everyone….. In a very short time Jack found he was really enjoying himself, and after about 20 minutes or so, Jack was really starting to relax when Jonathan Brisbane came over and told him that when he was a little older and had more practice against first-class players, he could see Jack going a lot further in the game and also that Jack would be a great credit to his father.

# CHAPTER 3

When their celebratory dinner in the Club House was finished, Jack and a few of his cohorts left and headed down the road to a pub/gaming club that another one of the lads had recommended. It was the first time Jack had been in a Casino, it was very full crowded with gamblers of all ages, and he was amazed by it all as he had only ever seen this sort of thing, croupiers and the like, on television. All the advice his dad had given him seemed to just vanish…. At the first table he came to, which was piled high with chips of different colours and were scattered all over the green baize in what looked like a hopeless muddle. But the Croupier definitely wasn't in a muddle, as she gave the big wheel a sharp turn. And then with what looked like a natural flick of her slim wrist, she threw in the small white ball, and after the ball spun round and round it plopped down on a number and stopped dead. There were a few yelps of delight from the onlookers, but they were drowned out by the moans of the punters who had lost their money, as a different croupier with an indifferent gesture raked in all of their lost chips. After observing the scene for a few more minutes Jack wandered over to another table, where they were playing a game called Trente et Quarante. He stood there watching the game closely, But, he just couldn't figure it out. As Jack glanced around the Casino he saw a small crowd assembled in the room over to his right, so, he confidently sauntered over and in. He was immediately conscious of the tension in the room….. There was a big game of Baccara being played, all the players were seated around an oval table, which had a large hole in the middle of it, and the dealer was standing in the middle of the table. There was also a brass rail encircling the entire table and it's purpose was to keep the players away from the bystanders, and Jack couldn't figure out how the players got in to sit at the table and play, or got back out when they needed to. There were actually nine players on each side of the table, with the dealer in the middle of the table and the croupier facing him, and the dealer it seems was a true professional. He was handling the game with swift dexterity. While Jack watched him closely, he realized that the dealer's eyes were trained on everything that was going on around the table, and while the expression on his face remained mute and inscrutable, it never changed whether the house won or lost. Jack was mesmerized by it all as he was a lad who had been thriftily brought up and it gave him a peculiar thrill to see someone risk a small fortune, or more probably a couple of thousand, which anyway was a small fortune to Jack, all on the turn of a card, and when they lost their money they made a spurious little joke and laughed. It was all terribly exciting. Just then Kyle came over to Jack and nudged him hard on his right shoulder before asking 'had any luck?' 'Me, oh no, I haven't been playing at any of the tables, just watching, what about you?' 'No, I'm not going to get fleeced' Kyle told him, 'come on, we're all going to the bar to have a drink.' On retiring to the bar and while they were having their drink's Jack told his pals that this was the first time he had ever been in a place like this. 'Oh, if that's the case then you must have a little flutter, you know, just to mark the occasion' Kyle continued sounding like a pro. 'Well my dad won't be too pleased when I tell him I was here' Jack told them, 'then don't tell him' Kyle smugly replied. And Jack left it at that, and finishing his bottle of beer he wandered back to the tables. He stood there for a while watching it all….. the loser's money being professionally raked in by the croupier and the winnings being paid out to the victor's. It all seemed to be done so smoothly and discreetly, and Jack found he couldn't take his eyes off the action. At the next table people were playing roulette, and again Jack watched with rapt attention. Maybe his pals had a point, he was here and it was his first time. Maybe it really would be an experience and maybe he shouldn't let this opportunity pass him by. Okay, so dad has advised me all about the perils of women and gambling, but I only agreed not to forget what he said, that was all. Jack took a crisp clean €50.note from his wallet, and feeling very Macho he put it down on the number 18, primarily because that was his age, but also because he didn't know what other number to use. Then the croupier turned the wheel with a definite twist and as Jack watched the white ball travelling around, his heart was thumping in his chest. The white ball seemed to hesitate, and just as it seemed to be about to stop it went on for another turn of the table before finally falling into one of the slots, Jack couldn't believe his eyes. **<u>No. 18.</u>** Suddenly a large multi coloured pile of chips was pushed across the table, it stopped directly in front of him. He was amazed, and then a moment later, the gentleman next to him slapped him hard on his back, loudly congratulating him on winning a second time. 'But how? I mean I didn't have a bet on?' 'Yes you had!' the gentleman with a laughing voice told him, 'your original stake was still on the table, they always leave it on the table until you ask for it back. You didn't know that, did you?' And another large pile of chips was pushed in front of him, joining the pile already there. Jack's head spun as he tried to count his winnings, and this time he asked to withdraw his winnings, thinking it imprudent to tempt fate with a third attempt, his total winnings now came to three thousand euro's. Jack who by now was in a state of joyous disbelief felt a sense of power, he also felt great, he felt as if he was invincible. None of his pal's had done this…. none… just him. Jack had never realized that he could make so much money so easily and so quickly, his dad would have to work for almost two months to make this type of money, or so he surmised. His face was wreathed in smiles, glancing around the table his eyes met those of a young lady who seemed to be staring at him. She was standing just a few feet away, to his right, she smiled over at him, and her smile showed him a set of pristine snow-white teeth, she kept her gaze fixed on him. 'Your luck's in this evening' she told him. Jack realized that while her English was very good, her accent certainly wasn't Irish, she sounded Italian or so he believed. 'I I know can you believe it?' Jack told her,' it's my first time ever playing, and it's also my first time ever being in a casino.' 'So, that explains it, beginner's luck! Now, could you be an Irish gentleman and lend me 200euro, you see I've managed to lose all my money. But, I will be able to give it back to you in half-an-hour or so, okay,' and without waiting for Jack's answer she bent over the table revealing her very impressive cleavage. She gathered up forty of the red chips from the pile he had in front of him and with barely a word of thanks or even a nod of acknowledgment, she put Jack's chips into her chip bucket, turned around and with a confident swish of her hips walked away from the table and away from Jack who was just standing there with his mouth hanging open. 'Oh, you'll never see those again young man,' the gentleman to his right told him. Jack was astounded….. It occurred to him that he had just committed a cardinal sin, at least it would be a cardinal sin in his father's eyes. But the fact was that Jack had never felt such all-consuming affection for the world around him, it had just never occurred to him to try to refuse her. *Oh well, I still have the rest of the money, I'll just have another shot at this or maybe even two, and if I don't win I'll pack up the rest of my winnings and leave. No matter what, it'll have been a great night.* So Jack put twenty red chips down on the green baize on top of the number seventeen, it was his sister's age, well if it worked once then maybe it will work again. But this time it didn't work. Next he tried his younger sister's age, but again it didn't work. *What am I doing wrong? Okay once more, just for luck.* This time he just picked a random number out of his head, and he won!…. The thrill came rushing back, and Jack figured that he should keep on playing. By now his three friends were watching him and they just couldn't believe what they were seeing. Time went on, and at the end of almost an hour Jack had won, and then lost back fairly large sums of money, a number of times. He decided that he had been playing long enough, so he gathered up the large pile of chips in front of him and with his two hands almost over flowing with chip's he quickly walked over to the changer's booth..... Jack gasped when the teller at the changer's booth fanned out ten thousand euro in crisp clean notes, and placed them on the green baize in front of him. His pals just stared at him their mouths hanging open, they were all too shocked to say a word. And all Jack was thinking was that he had never seen so much money in all his life. So, not really knowing what he should do now he hastily picked up the large bundle of notes, he seemed to be trying to press the large bundle of notes together, as if he were trying to reduce the size of the bundle, while at the same time, cramming the thick bundle of pristine notes into the zipped pocket in the lining of his jacket. Jack was turning away from the changer's booth when the young Italian woman who he had given the chips to earlier came rushing up to him. 'Oh I've been looking everywhere for you, I was beginning to think that you had left, and if you had then what must you be thinking of me?' She stated all of this in a very matter of fact voice and she seemed out of breath, 'here's the money you lent me and thank you so much for the loan, you've made my evening for me, so thanks.' Jack was blushing madly as he looked down at the lovely face, *well, dad told me not to gamble and looked what's happened. He also said not to have anything to do with young women but I did and I got a result. The fact is that I'm not nearly such a young fool as he think's.* Maybe not but Jack was totally taken aback by this young Italian woman, so much so that he seemed to be incapable of speech. She laughed lightly and in a husky concerned sounding voice asked Jack if he was okay, and Jack reddened even more to the roots of his rusty head of hair. 'Come on honey, talk to me,' she encouraged him in her husky voice 'tell me what's making you blush?' 'Well, to tell you the truth, I sort of never thought I would see that money, or you again, and I put it down to a lesson well learned.' 'My, aren't you a deep young man,' she told him with a smile, 'my name's Daniella and you are?' 'Jack, I'm Jack, '.... 'well, I'm just heading off now with my

pal's' he mumbled after a few moments of awkward silence.........
Daniella was dressed demurely for someone so young and nubile, she
had on a plain black woollen dress, with a neckline that definitely
accentuated her cleavage. Around her slim neck she wore a thin gold
link chain and it had an apostrophe shaped pendant that seemed to be
completely at home as it rested in the crevice of her ample breasts.
Jack felt something stir and found himself being drawn to her, he
guessed Daniella was two or three years older than him, but what of it
he found himself thinking. 'My fiancée is stuck in a game of poker
upstairs and I'm just wasting some time until he finishes up,'

# CHAPTER 4

He was turning away from the changer's booth when the young Italian woman came rushing up to him. 'Oh, I was looking everywhere for you, I was beginning to think that you had left, and if you had then what must you be thinking of me?', she stated all of this in a very matter of fact voice and she seemed out of breath, 'here's the money you lent me and thank you so much for the loan. You've made my evening for me, so thanks.' Jack was blushing madly as he looked down at her lovely face, *well, dad told me not to gamble and look what's happened. He also said not to have anything to do with young woman and I did. I used my judgment and I got a result. The fact is that I'm not nearly such a young fool as he think's*. Maybe not but Jack was totally taken aback by this young Italian woman, so much so that he seemed to be incapable of speech. She just laughed lightly, 'are you okay?' she asked in a husky, concerned voice, and Jack reddened even more to the roots of his rusty hair. 'Come on honey, talk to me,' she encouraged him in her husky voice 'tell me what's making you blush?' So Jack told her, 'well to tell you the truth, I sort of never thought I would see that money, or you again, and I put it down to a lesson well learned.' 'My, for a young man aren't you deep!' she told him with a smile, 'my name's Daniella and you are?' 'Jack, I'm Jack, and, I'm just heading off now with my pal's' Jack uttered after a few moments of silence…. Daniella was dressed demurely for someone so young and nubile, she had on a plain black wool dress but it did have a neckline that accentuated her cleavage. Around her slim neck she wore a thin gold link chain and it had an apostrophe shaped pendant that seemed to be completely at home resting in the crevice of her ample breasts. Jack felt himself being drawn to her, he guessed Daniella was only two or three years older than him, but what of it, he found himself thinking. 'My fiancée is stuck in a game of poker upstairs and I'm just wasting some time until he finishes up' she told Jack. 'Well, as I've said I'm just heading off with my pal's.' jack said not really knowing what else to say…. 'Sorry but didn't I see you playing in the tournament in Fitzwilliam Tennis Club earlier on this afternoon?' she coyly asked. 'Yes you sure did, but I don't know why you would have noticed me,' Jack responded in a puzzled sounding voice. 'Well, you got to the semi-finals in the doubles aren't I right? I watched that match, and I have to say I was very impressed by your style.' Now Jack wasn't usually cocky or a bullish sort of lad, quite the opposite in fact, but it did cross his mind that perhaps she'd borrowed the chips in order to become better acquainted with him. 'Do you ever go into Leeson Street to Claudine's' she asked. 'No, I never have,' Jack replied, his confidence in talking to her was starting to soar. 'Well, it had the most delicious bacon and egg's, and I'm starving.' She told him. His father's voice and all his emphatic warnings sounded in Jack's head, but Jack was sure his advice didn't or wouldn't apply here. Why, you only had to look at this pretty little thing to know without a shadow of a doubt that she was a nice respectable young woman. *Her fiancée is too busy playing card's to look after her, so I should. That's what mum would say.* After winning all of this money, Jack knew it couldn't possibly be a bad idea to have a little fun, so, 'okay, Claudine's it is, but I have to head home after that, I can't stay very long.' 'That's okay. We can leave when you're ready.' Jack thought that Claudine's was lovely, and he ate the bacon and egg's with relish, they shared a delicious bottle of Ontannon, a red wine that Daniella had chosen. There was smooth seductive music playing softly in the background, and the singer had a gorgeous, throaty voice and just before they left the club one of Jack's friends came over to him and quietly told him to be careful, but Jack just rolled his eyes at him. 'Has anyone ever told you that you're a very good looking young man Jack,? *Gosh, is she falling for me already?* With this his heart was speeding up at a ferocious pace, his desire for this woman seized him, and looking into her gorgeous face, hunger, longing, and desire were combined in one hot look, her proximity is exhilarating it's almost overwhelming. Then he began thinking that maybe *I shouldn't have drunk all that wine, I've never really been out drinking like that before,* and he realized this was the first piece of common-sense he had thought all night. The hour was getting on so, Jack decided that he had better make a move to go home or who knew where he was going to end up, now that his pals had been left behind in the club. And he knew that wouldn't go down well, if, and more likely when it got back to his dad. 'I'll shall go too,' Daniela resolutely told him, 'so you can drop me back to my hotel on your way.' Jack called for their bill and when it was presented he was rather shocked by the size of it, but with all of his winnings he knew it wasn't a problem and he left what he hoped was a good tip. When they got into a taxi outside the club, Daniella snuggled up to him….. Jack was surprised and he thought of the boyfriend she had left behind at the club, playing card's. *But I'm the man of the moment, like a classic romantic hero like like Sir Lancelot* he thought to himself with a sense of self satisfied confidence….. Obviously the wine was having its natural effect on him and the next moment Jack was placing his hand under her chin and lifting it up so that her full red lips moved to meet his, and she seemed to like it, *this really is my night, she want's to be here with me,* he confidently told himself. Daniella wasn't trying to pull away, she really seemed to be enjoying the kiss and Jack felt an intoxicating rush of happiness, *gosh I must be good at this* and she kept of kissing him. Her tongue shot into his mouth and Jack nearly gagged with the shock, but the shock only lasted for a second. Push and pull, attraction and fear were what he was feeling as he opened his eyes and looked at her lovely face. She seemed to be trying to get even closer to him, if that was possible as they were in the back seat of a taxi and there's really only so much room. Once they arrived at her hotel Daniella climbed out of the back seat, turned around and beckoned Jack with her long index finger to follow….. So eighteen year old Jack handed a bundle of notes to the cabbie and climbed out in as dignified a manner as he could. As he was closing the taxi door Jack was desperately trying to calm himself down. The very next moment he heard the word's 'well, I'll just head home now okay,' come out of his mouth, and he said it loud enough for Daniella to hear him, because by this time Daniella was half way up the steps to the front of the hotel, 'the walk and the air will do me good,' he said even though he wasn't too sure which direction he should be walking in. 'Darling you've been so good to me tonight, since we met actually, so why don't you come up to my room for a little while and I will show you just how grateful I am.' Daniella was talking down to Jack from the steps and while she was standing there a sudden gust of wind caught the hem of her dress and lifted it until it seemed as if it was dancing lightly around her shapely thighs. For a brief moment, Jack could see his Dad in his head, and he was just about to start dispensing his advice again….. So Jack put him firmly out of his head. *Okay I can do this*, he thought as various scenarios were filtering their mucky way thru his youthful mind, he was a fine young man, hear him roar, it was just too bad he felt more like a lion cub than a lion. Jack forgot all about his dad as he walked up the steps behind and went straight into the coffee coloured foyer, then Daniella and Jack sauntered over to lift, the door slid open and they entered and went straight up to the third floor, her floor. On leaving the lift they walked down a pristine corridor, it had those bland prints you find on nearly every hotel wall until they reached door No.18, the same as his age. They were no sooner inside the bedroom and Daniella turned and pulled him into her chest. She wrapped her arm's round his neck, raised her head and began kissing him passionately full on his lips, while at the same time she was gently rubbing the back of his neck in slow circular motions. To Jack it felt like little electric sparks were shooting off her fingers and her lips. He had never known that all the feelings and sensations that he felt coursing thru his body could be realised, but then again he's only eighteen and he has never been kissed like this before, or come to think of it, he had never been this alone at this late hour with a strange young woman. Oh yes! He had been kissed, but they had only ever been quickie kisses outside a youth club disco and as sure as he knew his name, he knew they couldn't be compared to this. This was a very real kiss, this part of his life is only in it's infancy. Daniella walked him over to the bed, kissing him all the way. Jack liked this, then, entwining her fingers she gently pulled his rusty hair forward, tipping his face down closer to her. Their tongues entwined deepening their kiss, as Jack moaned passionately. Daniella started opening his buttons, belts and zips and it felt as if her two hand's were everywhere and Jack felt an odd yet an exciting shiver run down his back. He just knew this was how it should feel when a young man's body wanted a young woman, and he felt such a giddy feeling, that here was where she wanted to be. With him. He could feel her heart beating so quickly, right up against his chest, then they both somehow managed to clamber into the bed.................. Jack exhausted and all as he was fell into a fitful sleep, he had never been a deep sleeper and the least little sound usually woke him up. So, when he woke up a few hours later, it took a few seconds for his sleepy brain to be able to tell him where he actually was, and what had actually transpired here. The bedroom wasn't totally dark as the bathroom door was ajar and the lights for some reason were on in there. All of a sudden jack was conscious of a body moving surreptitiously around the bedroom. Then he remembered it all, it was Daniela sneaking around the room. Jack was just about to say something to her when something about the way she was moving around stopped him. She was walking very slowly, as if she were afraid her movements would maybe wake him up, stopping dead still she looked over at Jack as he lay still as if he was asleep, she looked at his face very intently, but thankfully his eyes appeared to be closed and resting, he had only opened them slightly to see what was going on in the bedroom. Jack was starting to get really worried now and he was wondering what she was up to, he had never been in this sort of situation before now. Next, she tiptoed over to the chair where he had put his jacket to hang earlier, and once more she glanced over at him lying supposedly comatose in the bed. She waited for what seemed to Jack like an interminable time, the silence was so intense that Jack was sure he could hear his own heart beating and if he could hear it then surely she could also hear it as it pounded in the silence of the night. Then very slowly and very quietly Daniella pulled back the lapel of his jacket, slipped her hand inside and proceeded to draw out the thick bundle of notes that Jack had been so proud to win. Silently the lapel of the jacket fell back into place, so that it looked as if the jacket had never been disturbed, all the while she was holding onto the bundle of Jack's money in her left hand. Jack had to repress an instinctive impulse to jump up and grab her because the way he saw it, she was brazenly stealing his money. But it was partly the shock of the moment that kept him quiet and still, and also the fact that he was in a strange hotel in the middle of the night, and he wasn't sure what she was capable of doing, if he disturbed her. Looking over at him there was a cruel smile curving her lips. Then, when she had reassured herself that her movements hadn't disturbed his sleep, she stepped with infinite caution across the bedroom to a corner where there was a very realistic looking plastic plant in a large ceramic pot. Reaching down to the base of the main branch of the plastic plant and taking a firm hold of it, she easily lifted it out, and put it down on the floor beside the pot, then she put her left hand with the bundle of Jack's money in it down into the bottom of the large pot. And ever so quietly she replaced the plant back into the pot, Daniella stepped back, smiling as she admired her handiwork, it looked as is she had never touched it. So, creeping back across the bedroom she slipped back under the covers, and snuggled up against Jack's back almost as if she had never left the bed. 'Jack' she whispered, her voice was warm and silky. Jack breathed steadily almost as if he was immersed in a deep sleep. So Daniella turned over to the other side, and sighing contentedly she went off to sleep. Jack knew she was asleep by her gentle snoring. He was lying still, very still, but in the dark his thoughts were far from still, they were all over the place, *she's nothing but a dirty rotten thief, yes that's what she is, a dirty rotten thief, she played me like I would play a game of monopoly, so what do I do now?* After a few more moments and judging by her regular breathing, Jack was pretty confident that Daniella was really sound asleep. *Then again it's easy to fall asleep after a good night's work,* she thought sarcastically to herself. Jack couldn't believe what she had done to him. First she had relieved him of his virginity, and then she had relieved him of his winnings. And then after all that, she actually had the nerve to climb back into the bed and snuggle up to him. It infuriated Jack that she could rest so peacefully while he was lying there wide awake, his brain whirring trying to work out what he needed to do next.

# CHAPTER 5

S uddenly it came to him!

It is such a good idea especially for a still naïve 18-year old, that he was tempted to reach around and patted himself on the back, and he would have only he was afraid that he would mistakenly touch her face and wake her up. Jack waited for about ten minutes until Danielle's breathing was as smooth and as regular as a child in slumber. 'Daniella' he whispered, but there was no answer she appeared dead to the world. So, very slowly, pausing after each small movement Jack slid out of the bed, and Daniella seemed to be none the wiser as she lay there. Once out of the bed Jack standing upright stood back, stock-still and looked down at her breasts as they rose and fell with her regular and deep breathing. His movements didn't seem to have disturbed her, so he took a few steps and then waited, then he took a few more steps. It seems Jack is thankfully very light on his feet and so made absolutely no sound as he moved around the bedroom. It took him a few moments to get all the way across the room, without banging off something or tripping to the corner where the potted plastic plant was standing. Once there he stopped and waited again…..This time as he waited he heard the bed creak, but it was just Daniella turning over in her sleep. Jack forced himself not to move until he had counted to fifty, *yes, she's definitely sleeping like a baby,* so with infinite care reaching down he grabbed the plastic plant by its main stalk, and slowly pulled it up and out of the pot setting it down on the floor. Jack's heart was pounding twenty to the dozen as he reached down into the base plant pot. When his fingers touched the top of the bundle of bank notes that Danielle had deposited in there earlier he smiled, and when his hand closed tightly around the bundle of notes he slowly but proudly drew the notes out from the plant pot. Then Jack silently managed to replace the plastic plant into the pot without making a sound. He straightened himself up, turned, and quietly walked over to the chair where his jacket was hanging, while the whole time keeping one eye on Daniela as she lay on the bed. In his youthful opinion Daniela was a very deceitful female, and thankfully she remained stock-still as he placed his bundle of notes back into the breast pocket of his jacket, and his confidence was soaring as he quietly zipped it shut. Then cop on the utmost care not to rouse her he slowly got dressed, and his spirits were lifting as he thought of the great story he would have to tell to his college chums the next time they were all together, he was confident that nothing like this had ever happened to any of them. Now almost fully dressed he knew he had to get across the room without banging off of anything to get to the door. And somehow he had managed to do this so quietly that he wouldn't have disturbed even the lightest sleeper, or so he thought. But the door still had to be unlocked and that could pose a problem as he did remember the loud clicking noise it had made when they were coming in earlier. So while holding his breath, as if that would influence anything, he began turning the key slowly, it clicked, it seemed to click so loudly in the darkness of the night....

'Who's that?'

Daniela shot up in the bed keeping her back as straight as a rod, she somehow managed to keep her breasts covered with the sheet. Jack's heart jumped, into his mouth or so he thought, but he was relaxed once he realized that she was only half-awake. 'It's okay Daniela love, it's only me,' Jack whispered, 'listen to me now, lie back down or you will get cold. I'm sorry but I really have to go, I was trying not to wake you because you looked so peaceful lying there.' 'Oh, come over here, you silly boy and kiss me before you go,' and Jack honestly believed she was talking to him in her sleep. 'Please oh please… this has been such a memorable evening, you really are a lovely young man and you're also a great young lover, so, Bon Voyage.' With that Daniela lay back down in the bed with her two arm's outstretched waiting for him. Resistance was futile, or maybe it was just the easiest option. Jack went quickly over to the bed, bent down and planted a surprisingly luscious kiss on her full lips. He was very impressed with himself, and was even more so when he thought of what she had just said about him being a great lover, *well I must be a natural at this 'cause she didn't even realize that this was my first time and that she has just taken my virginity.* 'You really are a lovely guy, so again Bon Voyage.' and this was said with her two eyes firmly shut. Then after quietly slipping on his jacket he patted the pocket to make sure his bundle of money was still safely there.

Then he left room No.18. and headed down the corridor towards the lift's, by now Jack's imagination was working overtime, he was imagining her goon's jumping out of the wall's at him…..When he got to the foyer he proceeded to sit down in one of the plush chairs, the most discreet one, and put on his sock's and shoe's, the chap at the desk was eyeing him suspiciously, 'are you okay?' he asked banally. Jack finished lacing his shoe's up and stood up defiantly and walked out of the hotel without answering. It was light out but the street's were still still deserted except for a few late-night straggler's trying wearily to make their way home to their comfy beds. Jack took a long deep breath of the sweet early morning air, he was feeling as pleased as punch with himself, with what had gone down in the past few hours. Back in his room, Jack stepped into the hot shower and while the hot water was washing over his body, he was lathering himself his body with shower wash and proudly that he was not as big a mug as some people, namely, his dad might think….. He was towelling himself dry and his stomach started rumbling and he realized he was really famished. So once he was dried off and dressed he went down to the cafeteria for some breakfast. It wasn't a continental breakfast like he usually had, this time it was a full on Irish breakfast, bacon, eggs and warm roll's fresh from their oven's, so crisp and delicious they melted in your mouth, and a small pot of very hot Barry's tea. It was so unusual for Jack not to have to count his money before ordering, but now he had all of his winning's. His full Irish arrived in no time and while he was eating it he was thinking what he should do with all of this money.

When Jack is finished his breakfast he went back to his own room, he turned the lock on his bedroom door because he had decided to lay out all of the notes and count them, and try to devise a plan of what to do with it. He had so nearly lost the notes, that they seemed to have taken on a much greater value for him. He unzipped his breast pocket, and took the note's out spreading them on his desk in a fan shape. To his immense surprise instead of there being 10,000€ in the bundle, there was 11.500€. Not quite believing what he was seeing, his two eye's were bulging just like a pig's on steroids, he couldn't understand it. Hastily gathered them up into a thick pile he proceeded to count them again, even asking himself if it was possible that he had won more than he had realized. But NO, that was out of the question, he was sure he could remember the cashier at 'Claudine's' counting out each and every note. Suddenly, it came to him, it had been dark in the room when he was taking the notes from the base of the plastic plant pot, and there was probably some of Daniela's own money in the pot as well. The plant-pot must have been her money box, and Jack had taken back not only his own money, but her money as well.

The thief becomes the victim!

*Where oh where are my pal's, this really is unbelievable, I have sex, I lose my virginity and it turn's out that she is a pro, and I manage to make money off her….. I really should make this into a book, it will be the next best-seller.* Then he thought of her going to the plant-pot later that morning, expecting to find all of the money she had so deceptively acquired, and finding it was all gone, even her own money was gone as well.

Jack burst out laughing….. There was nothing he could do about it, he knew neither her surname, or the name of the hotel to which she had taken him, he couldn't return her money, not even if he wanted to. 'Oh well, it serves her damned well right' he said out loud.

This was the story Raymond O'Keefe related to his friends over the bridge table later that week. He went on to tell them that after dinner the previous evening while Susan was in the kitchen helping the girls with their home-work Jack had narrated it in detail + full blown colour to him. 'And do you know what he said to me when he was finished with his story, looking at me with those big innocent eyes of his, he said, Dad, do you remember the advice you gave to me just before I left to go to university? You told me not to gamble, well, I did and I made a small fortune, next you told me I was to have nothing to do with women, young or not so young, well, I did, and by doing so I made even more money.' It didn't make it any better for Raymond when all of his good friend's burst out laughing at what he had just told them. 'Less of the laughing now, please, I'm in a very sticky situation and I could do with some good advice. Jack used to look up to me, he used to respect me and took whatever I said as the gospel, and now I'm getting the feeling that he look's on my opinion as just the rambling's of an old fool who's past it. It's no use me telling him that it was a one off, he refuses to see it as a fluke, I'm honestly worried that he thinks the whole thing was due to his own brilliance and I'm worried, because I honestly think it will do him no good thinking like this, it just might be his undoing.'

'Well Raymond 'one of his pals started in a serious voice 'he did make you look like a bit of a fool, there's really no denying that now is there?' Raymond responded in a quiet voice 'I know, and I don't like it

I mean in all reality my advice was sound.' 'No one is disputing that Raymond, it was undoubtedly sound advice and we've probably all given much the same sort of advice to our own kids down thru the year's,' at this statement all of them around the table nodded their head's in agreement. 'And now instead of learning a lesson I'm afraid Jack's not going to listen to anything I have to say in the future. So, if any of you experienced fathers can advise me on how I'm to deal with him from now on, I will really be very grateful.' 'Well Raymond if I were you I wouldn't be getting too worried,' said one of his oldest friends 'my view on this type of situation is this: in view of what you've just told us, your Jack seems to have been born lucky, and in the long game of life that's much better and in my opinion will serve him much better than if he had been born, either clever, or into a wealthy family.'

he End.